The Animal Adventure

·A HELLO KITTY ADVENTURE·

HarperCollins *Children's Books*

MEET

Hello Kitty
and friends

Hello Kitty

Mimmy

Tammy

Mama

Papa

Grandpa

Grandma

Fifi

Dear Daniel

With special thanks to
Linda Chapman and Michelle Misra

First published in Great Britain by HarperCollins *Children's Books* in 2014

www.harpercollins.co.uk
1 3 5 7 9 10 8 6 4 2
ISBN: 978-0-00-754067-9

Printed and bound in England by Clays Ltd, St Ives plc.

MIX
Paper from
responsible sources
FSC® C007454

Contents

Off on Holiday

Hello Kitty bounced up and down in the back of the car. On one side of her Tammy was reading a book and on the other side, Fifi was drawing a picture, but Hello Kitty was so excited she couldn't sit still! Dear Daniel was sitting in the front of the car. He kept turning round to talk to her. Dear Daniel, Fifi and Tammy were Hello Kitty's three **best** friends. Together, they had started a club called The Friendship Club. They liked to make things and bake, have sleepovers and go to places

they'd never been before – and now they were going away together for two **whole** nights!

Dear Daniel's father, who was driving the car, told them that they only had a little way to go. Not long to wait now!

Hello Kitty felt like she would burst with

happiness. They were off to stay in the

countryside with Dear Daniel's aunt. She had

recently bought Willow Farm – a farm with

four holiday cottages, a swimming pool, and

lots of friendly animals. She had asked The

Friendship Club to come and stay with her

to help look after the animals, and to get all the preparations done before her first holiday guests arrived. The Friendship Club had looked at photos of the farm on the internet and it looked **AMAZING!**

Hello Kitty had made a list of all the things she wanted to do...

- Groom the ponies
- Feed the ducks
- Go swimming
- And most importantly be VERY helpful!

There was going to be lots to do, but Hello Kitty loved helping people. It was one of her favourite things to do!

The car turned off the main road and soon they were driving through some **very** narrow country lanes with high hedges on each side. A couple of times another car came in the other direction and they had to stop to let them pass, but finally they reached a driveway that had a big sign on it saying WILLOW FARM.

The Friendship Club cheered! This was it — they were here **at last!** They drove up the long driveway through some woods. As they came out of the trees they could see the

Hello Kitty and friends

farmhouse and four cottages, as well as a big

pond. Dear Daniel said he wanted to go for a

paddle in the pond; Fifi wanted to *run* round

the fields; Tammy wanted to go and explore

the cottages, and Hello Kitty wanted to see the

animals. Dear Daniel's dad laughed and told them he couldn't drive if they all made so much noise! They all shushed a bit, but it was just too exciting to be quiet!

As they pulled in to park, Dear Daniel's aunt came out to greet them with a dog with a sandy-coloured coat bounding at her heels. The Friendship Club tumbled out of the car to pat him, as she told them the dog was called Rufus and he was very friendly. He wagged his tail and tried to lick them all.

They listened hard as they were told where they'd

be sleeping, and where everything was. Dear

Daniel's aunt showed them up to their bedroom

on the top floor, and left them to it – she said

Dear Daniel could show them around, as he

had been to the farm before on a day trip. It

was a **massive** room with

four beds and their own

bathroom, and through the

windows they could see

out over the fields and

woods. They put their

suitcases on their beds

but Hello Kitty, Tammy

and Fifi didn't want to

waste time unpacking – they wanted to go and

explore! Dear Daniel smiled. That was

great, but how about a snack first? They must

be hungry and thirsty after their long drive –

because he definitely was! The girls giggled,

and followed him downstairs. The kitchen was

large and cosy with a rug on the floor and a
huge pine table with chairs all around it. There
was a jug of orange juice, a big plate of home-
made scones, a pot of cream and a pot of jam
on the table. Dear Daniel told everyone to help
themselves so they all sat down and dug in! The
scones were YUMMY and Rufus loved eating
all the scraps!

While they ate, Dear Daniel explained that his aunt needed to spend the next two days putting the final touches to the cottages and garden, so was hoping The Friendship Club would be able to make sure all the animals were ready and their

stables and pens cleaned out. She had given Dear Daniel a list of things to do – what did they think? He looked round nervously. Everyone **smiled** and nodded. They wanted to help out as much as they could!

When they had finished eating they cleared away and Dear Daniel gave them a tour of the farm. Rufus *bounded* along beside them. The cottages were to one side of the farm with a big grass area in front of them for playing games on. Behind the cottages, a path led to the animals' fields and a fenced-in duck pond.

In the first field there was a sweet little white goat who tried to chew their sleeves and a mother sheep with two *adorable* lambs.

Next was a big wire enclosure full of hens that squawked and fluttered their wings as Dear Daniel took the girls in and showed them how to collect the eggs from their nesting boxes.

The next field was Hello Kitty's favourite – it had a dark brown donkey called Jenny in it, and a little Shetland pony called Minnie who had an orangey-brown coat and a **lovely** thick mane and tail. She had very cheeky eyes that

peeped up at them through a long forelock that

fell over her face like a fringe.

Both Jenny and Minnie were **very** friendly

but Dear Daniel warned them that Minnie

could be naughty. She liked to escape! She had

worked out how to undo the lock on her field

gate so she could go exploring around the farm.

His aunt now had a chain around the gate to

stop her. *Everyone* had to be very careful

about keeping it fastened because if there was a

way out, Minnie would be sure to find it!

Hello Kitty stroked the little pony. Dear

Daniel looked at his list, and saw that Minnie

pulled a little cart that was in one of the barns.

One of their jobs was to clean it up and paint it so children could have rides around the farm. That sounded fun!

After the pony field there was another field with some sheep and then the woods. Dear Daniel's aunt had warned them not to go playing in the woods on their own; the paths were **very** overgrown at the moment. She had some gardeners coming in on Monday but until then the woods were too dangerous because there were hidden ditches. No one minded staying out of the woods though. It looked like

there was going to be *more* than enough for

them to do on the farm!

Dear Daniel finished the

tour by showing them the

swimming pool. It was

indoors with big windows

all around it, and the water glinted a perfect blue. Fifi sighed; it looked just *perfect* for jumping into.

Dear Daniel smiled. There was a task at the bottom of the list from his aunt that he thought they might like

— don't forget to have fun! Maybe they could start by going for a swim? They all looked at each other, and broke into big grins. There was only one answer to that — YES PLEASE!

A Fun Evening

Hello Kitty, Dear Daniel, Fifi and Tammy had a wonderful swim in the pool. They pulled each other around on a big floating bed and took it in turns to dive under the water to pick up diving sticks.

When they had swum enough, they got
dressed and Dear Daniel's aunt showed them
how to feed the animals. There was a **lot** to
remember – the hens had grain; the goat and
the sheep had some dried green pellets; Minnie
the pony and Jenny the donkey had hay and
Rufus had dog food in a bowl.

After they had fed the animals Hello Kitty asked if there was anything else they could do to help that afternoon. There wasn't much time before tea but they could clean Minnie's leather bridle and harness…

Dear Daniel's aunt **smiled** and settled them down with cleaning things and some big buckets of warm water, and told them what to do. Then she went off to put up some curtains in one of the cottages and start the barbecue going for their dinner!

Cleaning Minnie's things was fun! First they had to spray a cleaner on to the saddle, and wipe that off with sponges dipped in warm water. Then they had to rub saddle soap into the leather – rubbing it until it *gleamed.* Dear Daniel was in charge of polishing the metal buckles and rings so that they shone brightly. As they worked, they all talked about the farm. They had already chosen their favourite animals – Dear Daniel liked Jenny the donkey, Tammy liked the lambs, Fifi liked Rufus the dog, and Hello Kitty liked Minnie the pony.

As they finished the cleaning, Fifi washed her sponge out in the bucket of water and tried to throw it on to the shelf where the cleaning things were kept. But...

Whoops! It missed and landed on Tammy's head! Tammy squealed as water dripped all over her.

35

Fifi clapped a hand over her mouth and said sorry straightaway, but then a loud giggle escaped from her mouth. Tammy did look quite funny!

Tammy's eyes glinted. She picked up the sponge and threw it back at Fifi; it sploshed into

Fifi's leg, leaving a big wet mark. Fifi dunked

it in the water and threw it back. But Tammy

ducked and it hit Hello Kitty instead!

Soon all four of them were having an

enormous water fight! They ran out

of the room, dodging and ducking and throwing

dripping sponges at each other. They ended up almost as wet as they had been when they had come out of the swimming pool!

When the water in the bucket finally ran out they were all pink in the face, but with big **smiles.**

They cleared the mess away and checked all the animals had fresh water. By the time they had finished they were dry again and it was time to eat.

They washed their hands and *ran* to the back garden of the farmhouse, where there were sausages and beef burgers sizzling on

the barbecue with Dear Daniel's aunt and dad

looking after them. They sat down around the

garden table, **munching** on their food and

drinking lemonade. The sun was starting to go

down but it was still warm and light outside – a

perfect summer evening.

As they ate, Dear Daniel looked at the list of things they needed to do while they were at the farm. They still had to...

- Clean out the sheep and goat's shelter
- Polish and paint Minnie's cart
- Bath and groom Minnie and Jenny
- Walk and bath Rufus

Would they be able to do all that? The Friendship Club all looked at each other – they were sure they could!

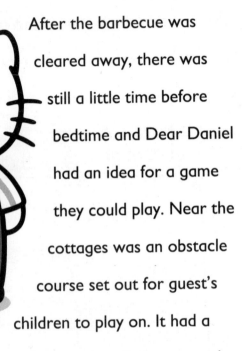

After the barbecue was cleared away, there was still a little time before bedtime and Dear Daniel had an idea for a game they could play. Near the cottages was an obstacle course set out for guest's children to play on. It had a hoop to go through, jumps to climb over and crawl under, and a tunnel to wriggle through. Hello Kitty, Fifi and Tammy jumped up and down with *excitement* – they all liked doing obstacle courses! Dear Daniel smiled and explained that this was going to be even more **fun** than a normal obstacle course! They were going to get into partners; then one person would be blindfolded and the other would guide them round the course. They all agreed that the game sounded like LOADS of fun! Super!

Hello Kitty paired up with Dear Daniel, and Fifi and Tammy went together. It felt **very** strange to have the blindfold on.

When Dear Daniel was guiding Hello Kitty, she took tiny steps and went slowly so she wouldn't fall

over. When it was Dear Daniel's turn to be

blindfolded he tried to go too *fast* and kept

bumping into things. They soon realised that

to get round quickly, the person doing the

guiding had to give very clear directions and the

person who was blindfolded had to listen hard

and do **exactly** what they were told.

They each had two goes at it and they were all

much better the second time round when they

worked together like a team. After they had

played for a while, Fifi yawned, Tammy yawned,

and then Dear Daniel and Hello Kitty joined in.

It was time to go and brush their teeth and get into their pyjamas so that tomorrow they could be up early. There was going to be **lots** to do! The Friendship Club grinned at each other – they couldn't wait!

Helping Out!

Hello Kitty was the first to wake up in the

morning. She bounced out of bed and pulled

open the curtains, and the sunlight streamed in.

Outside, the sky was blue with little white puffy

clouds floating across it and Hello Kitty could

see Minnie and Jenny down in the field.

She woke the others up and they all got dressed. As they put their clothes on, they started to talk about what order they would do the jobs in. The first job was *easy* – the animals all needed their breakfasts. But after that they all wanted to do different things. Fifi wanted to take Rufus for a walk and give him a bath; Dear Daniel wanted to clean up Minnie's cart; Tammy wanted to clean out the goat and sheep shelter and Hello

Kitty wanted to bath and groom Minnie and Jenny. *Hmmm...* what to do? Maybe they could decide after breakfast!

They hurried downstairs, where bacon, sausages and eggs were waiting for them to have after they had fed and watered the animals. The Friendship Club ran outside into the sun.

It was great fun putting the feed into the buckets and giving it all out. The sheep bleated, the hens clucked, Minnie whinnied and Jenny gave a loud EE-YORE! Hello Kitty stroked

Minnie and Jenny as they ate. She really hoped

she could persuade the others to start the jobs

by bathing and grooming Minnie and Jenny.

But after they had fed the animals and were

eating their own breakfast, the Friendship Club

still couldn't decide where to start!

They stood by the fields, all wanting to start with something *different*. Fifi thought Rufus needed a walk before his bath, and Dear Daniel said the cart would take a long time to dry when they painted it so they should get started on it early. Tammy thought the sheep

shelters really needed cleaning out, and Hello Kitty put in that if they were going to bath Minnie and Jenny they should do it while it was ᏚᏌᏁᏁᎩ and warm!

They simply couldn't agree so in the end they all decided to do different things. That way they could all do what they wanted!

It seemed like a good plan but
when Hello Kitty fetched
the warm water and
shampoo and tied
Minnie up, she couldn't
help *wishing*
that the others were
there to help her wash
the pony. Minnie nuzzled her.
It was lovely to fuss over her and rub shampoo
in her tail, but Hello Kitty kept thinking of how
much more fun it had been the night before
when they had been cleaning and doing the
obstacle course together as a group.

As she went to refill her water buckets, Hello Kitty saw Tammy wiping her arm across her forehead as she filled a bucket up with dirty straw. It looked like **hard** work. She wished she could go and help her, but she knew she couldn't leave Minnie with shampoo in her coat and there was still Jenny to wash too!

Dear Daniel was by the tap washing a paintbrush out. He'd cleaned the cart and started to paint it but it was a very fiddly job; it was going to take him ages!

Hello Kitty and friends

Hello Kitty said that washing Jenny and Minnie was going to take a long time, too. She hadn't realised how much shampoo she would use and how **many** water buckets she was going to need. She had thought about asking Dear Daniel to help her, but she didn't like to now that she saw how busy he was with his painting.

Hello Kitty sighed and carried the water buckets back to Minnie's field on her own. She started on Minnie's mane. As she

rubbed shampoo in, she saw Fifi

walking across the fields. Rufus

was bounding about happily

but Fifi was looking a bit

hurried. Hello Kitty wished

they were together. Oh, why

had they started the different

jobs on their own? It would have been much

more fun – and quicker – to work together.

The Friendship Club worked so hard all

morning that they didn't get a chance to talk

at all. By lunchtime they were feeling *very*

worn out! Dear Daniel's aunt had left them

a picnic blanket with an enormous plate of

sandwiches, some crisps and crispy apples, and

some lemonade to drink.

It was **hot** outside so Tammy suggested

they eat their picnic in the hay barn where it

was shady. They laid everything out on the hay

bales and tucked in. Sitting down for a while and having some food made them all feel better, and everyone started to chatter at once – asking each other how they were getting on.

Hello Kitty told her friends she had finished bathing Minnie and Jenny but that they would still need a good brush once their coats were dry – and she wanted to plait Minnie's mane, too! She'd found some pink ribbon in the stables and thought Minnie would look very *sweet* with it plaited into her hair.

They could **even** decorate the cart with it too when it was painted!

Dear Daniel declared that it was just about done – it was drying in the sun, but he also

wanted to polish the wheels. Tammy had cleaned out the goat and sheep shelter but she still needed to put some fresh straw down. Fifi had walked Rufus but still needed to bath him. It seemed like there were still **lots** of jobs for each of them to finish off.

Hello Kitty sighed as she thought about them all going off on their own again for the afternoon.

61

This wasn't how she had imagined the weekend *at all...*

They cleared the remains of lunch away and then went back to finish their jobs. Hello Kitty walked slowly to Minnie and Jenny's field, but frowned as she got to the gate. Where was Minnie? She could see Jenny but the little pony was nowhere to be seen.

Hello Kitty checked the gate but she had remembered to put the chain around it and it was still fastened. Minnie **couldn't** have escaped that way! She looked all around the field... and then she saw something that made her gasp in alarm! One of the wooden bars of the fence had fallen down and there was a gap just big enough for a naughty little pony to squeeze through...

Oh no! Hello Kitty's heart skipped a beat as she stared at the hole. Minnie must have escaped!

4

Where's Minnie?

Hello Kitty *raced* away to find the

others. Dear Daniel was checking the painting

he had done on the cart, but as soon as Hello

Kitty told him what was wrong he ran to get Fifi

while Hello Kitty got Tammy. They all hurried

down to the gap in the fence in Minnie and Jenny's field.

Dear Daniel looked closely at the broken fence and spotted some long golden tail hairs. **Oh no!** Hello Kitty was right; Minnie must have escaped that way. Tammy and Fifi propped up the fallen bar of wood so that it blocked the hole in case Jenny tried to escape too. Hello Kitty and Dear Daniel looked all around. Where had the pony gone?

Just then, Hello Kitty cried out as she spotted some hoof prints on the path. Minnie must have gone that way! They all ran along the path in the direction the prints were heading. Hello Kitty's heart beat fast. She hoped they would find Minnie soon. She was glad they weren't near a road so the pony wouldn't be in danger of being run over. Hopefully she would be OK – but **where** was she?

Fifi pointed as she saw some more hoof prints leading into the woods. Everyone stopped as they remembered that they shouldn't go into the woods because they were so overgrown. What should they do?

What if Minnie was in trouble?

Fifi suggested that she run back

and fetch the grown-ups. Everyone

agreed – Fifi was the *fastest*

runner of them all! The others would

go a little way into the woods just to

see if they could find Minnie, but they

wouldn't go out of sight of the field until

the adults got there.

Fifi turned and ran off.

The others walked forward carefully. The brambles and bushes grew thickly on every side, their branches snaking across the path. It was very dim, with the thick trees blocking out the sunlight. Roots stuck up through the ground, tripping them up.

They all called Minnie's name, and listened. Hello Kitty heard a whinny to the left. **Shhh!** They all stopped. Hello Kitty called Minnie's name again and they heard another whinny. She must be close by!

Tammy ran to the left side of the path where some of the bushes were broken and trampled. Minnie must have gone that way! They held hands and very carefully followed the trail.

THERE!

Hello Kitty could see the little pony. She was stuck in a big ditch! Minnie must have tried to trot across it without realising it was

a ditch because of all the brambles covering it. They could just see her head and ears as she struggled and tried to get out. ***Poor Minnie!***

Hello Kitty wanted to run to her but Dear Daniel grabbed her arm. They had to be careful — they didn't want to fall into a ditch themselves! They held hands and slowly walked forward.

Luckily there were no other ditches nearby and they **soon** reached Minnie. She whinnied as they got close. She had brambles wrapped around her legs and tangled in her tail and in the halter she was wearing. She looked very unhappy. She tried to push and pull her way out, kicking backwards and forwards, but the brambles held her fast.

Hello Kitty looked round. She hoped Fifi and the grown-ups would get there soon but there was no sign of them yet. She and Tammy and Dear Daniel were on their own.

Dear Daniel looked at the brambles. **Maybe** if they could untangle them, Minnie would be able to get out? But they couldn't do that if she was struggling because she might kick them. Could they calm her down?

Tammy had an apple in her pocket from lunch, so she handed it to Hello Kitty, who fed Minnie bites of it and stroked her face. It seemed to calm her down. Minnie stared at Hello Kitty with **big** brown eyes, as Hello Kitty whispered to her that everything was going to be OK. While she stroked Minnie, Tammy and Dear Daniel reached down into the ditch and started to pull the brambles away from Minnie's legs and tail.

Hello Kitty untangled some from Minnie's

mane and halter too, until finally she was totally

free from the brambles.

Now they just had to get her out of the ditch.

But **how** could they do that?

Hello Kitty *and friends*

Hello Kitty held some more apple in front of Minnie's nose to try and tempt her out. The pony tried to get out of the ditch, but she kept slipping back in! She wasn't going to be able to get out on her own.

Hmmm... What could they do? Then Dear Daniel had an idea. He had seen some long pieces of rope at the edge of the wood which had been tied around hay bales. They weren't far – he could run back and pick them up. Maybe they could use them and help pull her out?

Hello Kitty soothed Minnie as Dear Daniel
ran off and got the rope. When he came back
he slipped the rope through Minnie's halter.
Hello Kitty held out the last of the apple to her,
and then – *pull!* She and Tammy and Dear
Daniel all took hold of the rope.

As Minnie tried to get to

the apple, they pulled with all their might. It was

hard work! The rope dug into their hands and

Minnie's front hooves scrambled up

the bank. They *heaved* and

tugged as she scrabbled and

kicked. Hello Kitty gasped for

breath. She could see Minnie

was almost out! If only they

could pull a bit harder...

Just then they heard

Fifi calling out. They yelled to

her and she came running

through the trees,

bounding lightly over the

80

roots and brambles. She saw what they were

doing and grabbed hold of the rope too.

One… two… **_THREE!_**

With a final heave from all four of them,

Minnie scrambled out of the ditch!

They'd done it! Minnie was **free!**

Dear Daniel's aunt and dad came running

through the trees just as Minnie got out of the

ditch. They stopped in astonishment, and Dear

Daniel quickly explained what had happened.

His aunt ran over and checked Minnie, and the

little pony was *fine.* She was nudging Hello

Kitty with her nose, wondering what all the fuss

was about.

Dear Daniel's dad couldn't believe how quick-thinking the Friendship Club had been. They'd saved the day!

Hello Kitty hugged Minnie. She was just very, very glad sweet little Minnie was safe!

5

Having Fun... Together!

Hello Kitty led Minnie back to her field. Dear

Daniel's dad and aunt mended the hole in the

fence and then checked the rest of the fence

was strong and sturdy, while Dear Daniel,

Tammy and Fifi groomed Minnie and got the

remaining brambles out of her fur and tail. Jenny

wanted some fuss, too, and so they brushed her

and put some oil on her feet. By the time they

had finished, the pony and donkey both looked

beautiful!

The Friendship Club went off to help each other finish the rest of their jobs. They polished the wheels of the cart and decorated it with ribbons; they gave Rufus his bath, and had a **great** time shaking up the clean straw for a lovely fresh bed for the sheep and goat.

When they had finished all their jobs, there were delicious ice creams for them from Dear Daniel's aunt to say thank you for all their hard work! Yum! They sat down by the duck pond to lick their melting ice creams, and talked about rescuing Minnie. They were all so glad they had managed to pull her out when they did – it had been so hard to see her stuck in

that ditch! As they talked, Hello Kitty thought about how well they had all worked as a team to help Minnie. In fact, thinking about how they had done it gave Hello Kitty an idea for a new Friendship Club rule. She held up her hands to quiet everyone down, and announced it:

Good friends can do anything when they pull together!

She looked around at Fifi, Tammy and Dear

Daniel – what did everyone think? They all

grinned at each other. They **loved** it!

Oooh! Fifi grinned even wider and suggested

that they test out their new rule – by going

to the swimming pool and pulling each other

around on the giant floating bed! They all

agreed straightaway. One thing they had

Hello Kitty and friends

definitely learned that day — it was far more fun  when they did things together!

The rest of the time at Willow Farm *flew* by. All too soon the Friendship Club was packing up to go home. The farm looked

wonderful — the cottages were all ready for

guests, the animals were washed and clean, and

their shelters bedded down with fresh straw.

Minnie was hitched up to her freshly-painted

cart. There were pink ribbons in her mane and

harness, and tied to the back of the cart. She

was ready to give rides.

The first group of guests arrived and headed towards the cottages, with excited children pointing at the animals as they walked past. Hello Kitty *ran* over to say goodbye to Minnie. As the little pony nuzzled her, she kissed her nose and promised she would see her again soon.

Hello Kitty heard her name being called and turned to see Dear Daniel, Fifi and Tammy beckoning to her from the car park. It really

was time to go. Hello Kitty gave Minnie one **last** hug and then ran to join her friends.

Hello Kitty and friends

It was time to go home for now but one day they would be back – back for lots more fun together at Willow Farm!

The end

Turn over the page for activities and
fun things that you can do with your
friends – just like Hello Kitty!

Woolly Wonders!

Hello Kitty and the Friendship Club loved going to the farm to meet the animals. But if you can't go to the farm, you can still have some farmyard friends to play with, by making a whole flock of these sheep —
Baa-rilliant!

You will need:

- Newspaper
- Pen
- Masking tape
- Black drinking straws
- Black and white card or stiff paper
- Cotton wool balls
- Glue
- Scissors

MAKE SURE YOU ASK MAMA OR PAPA TO HELP!

Now – let's get crafty!

1. Scrunch up some newspaper into a ball!
   When you have a ball, wind the masking
   tape around it until it completely covers
   the newspaper, and gives you a nice round
   shape. This will be your sheep's body.

2. To make legs, cut four equal lengths of
   black drinking straw. Push four holes into
   the ball where the legs will go (use your
   pen), and insert the straws. Try to keep
   them even so your sheep can stand up!

3. Now glue your cotton wool balls on to
   your sheep's body. Stick them all over until
   it's completely covered.

4. Make your sheep's face. Copy the templates below and cut them out of your card. Make sure they're the right size for the body!

5. Now, draw a big dot in the middle of each piece of white card – these will be your eyes!

6. Glue the face together and then stick it on the front of your sheep. Ta da – your very own farmyard friend!

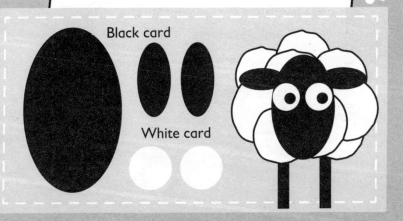

Black card

White card

Perfect Planting!

Even if you don't live on a farm, you can still grow your very own flowers, just like Hello Kitty!

MAKE SURE YOU ASK MAMA OR PAPA TO HELP!

You will need:

- A plant pot, window box, or a space in a flowerbed outside
- Soil or compost
- A trowel
- Seeds
- A watering can

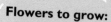

Flowers to grow:
These flowers are pretty, and easy to grow!
Pansies
Sunflowers
Sweet peas
Marigolds

1. Ask your grown-up to buy the seeds for your chosen plant.
2. Next, fill up your pot or box with soil, or dig a hole in your spot outside! Check the seed packet to see how deep the hole should be.
3. Cover your seeds with soil, and water them. Don't forget to water them regularly; two or three times a week should be enough.
4. Wait... and watch as your plants come to life!

The Prettiest Pots!

You can make your flowers even lovelier by decorating the pot you keep them in. Try some of Hello Kitty's tips for the prettiest pots around...

- Paint designs on your pots with acrylic paint in bright colours; you can even match them to your flowers!
- Glue on pretty pebbles or shells.
- Make a bow out of sturdy ribbon and glue it on to your pot.

After your flowers have bloomed, why not decorate the pot and give the plant to someone as a present? Like a living bouquet of flowers!

Turn the page for a sneak peek at

and friends'

next adventure...

The Halloween Parade

Hello Kitty smiled as she spread out a checked rug on the grass. Today was going to be perfect. She hadn't seen her friends Tammy and Fifi for a while, because it had been the school holidays and they had all been busy. That afternoon they were coming over for a picnic and she couldn't wait to catch up!

Quickly, she placed the little paper plates and cups on the rug, then she wound some pink fairy lights around the trunk of the apple tree.

Mama smiled at her as Hello Kitty ran back inside to get the food. She'd been wondering where she'd got to.

Hello Kitty picked up the jug of fruit punch and a plate of sandwiches from the table and put them carefully on a tray as she explained that she'd just been making sure everything was just right for her friends. Fifi and Tammy would be there any minute.

Mama balanced some rainbow-iced cupcakes on top of the tray too. Hello Kitty wouldn't want to forget those!

Hello Kitty grinned and thanked her, trying to keep everything steady as she made her way back outside.

Tammy and Fifi were two of Hello Kitty's best friends in the world, along with her twin sister, Mimmy, and her oldest friend, Dear Daniel. Dear Daniel was away at the moment travelling with his dad, a photographer. He'd been gone for the last two weeks. Hello Kitty smiled as she thought about Tammy, Fifi and Dear Daniel. They were all in the same class at school and had started the Friendship Club. They met at each other's houses to do fun things, like drawing, painting and baking.

Hello Kitty heard the doorbell ring and ran back inside. She threw the door open.

What a surprise! Tammy had a plate of biscuits and Fifi was carrying a big bowl of red jelly covered with sprinkles.

Hello Kitty had told her friends not to bring anything! But she didn't mind that they had. She happily gave them both a hug.

Tammy and Fifi smiled. They knew Hello Kitty would have had everything for them, but they wanted to bring something anyway.

Hello Kitty led them through the house to the garden, so they could see what she had ready for them. She showed them out into the garden, then stepped aside so they could see what she had set up. Ta da!

Fifi and Tammy gasped.

It was beautiful! They both laughed, and gave Hello Kitty another hug. They had missed her so much.

Hello Kitty laughed too, and poured them each a drink as she asked them about their holidays. What had they both been doing?

Find out what happens next in...

Coming soon!

The Halloween Parade
·A HELLO KITTY ADVENTURE·

The TV Star
·A HELLO KITTY ADVENTURE·

The Big Race
·A HELLO KITTY ADVENTURE·

The Makeover Party
·A HELLO KITTY ADVENTURE·

The Animal Adventure
·A HELLO KITTY ADVENTURE·

Collect all of the Hello Kitty and Friends Stories!

The Friendship Club

The School Trip

The Summer Fair

The Pop Princess

The Wedding Day

The Beach Holiday

The Treasure Hunt

The Talent Show

The Christmas Present
TWO SPECIAL CHRISTMAS STORIES

Christmas Special: Two Stories in One! •••••▶